Baby Beluga: Words and music by Raffi and Debi Pike. Text copyright © 1980, 1983 by Homeland Publishing, a division of Troubadour Records. Illustrations copyright © 1990 by Ashley Wolff.

Down by the Bay: Text copyright © 1987 by Troubadour Learning, a division of Troubadour Records Ltd. Illustrations copyright © 1987 by Nadine Bernard Westcott.

Everything Grows: Text copyright © 1989 by Troubadour Learning, a division of Troubadour Records Ltd. Illustrations copyright © 1989 by Bruce McMillan.

Five Little Ducks: Text copyright © 1989 by Troubadour Learning, a division of Troubadour Records Ltd. Illustrations copyright © 1989 by Jose Aruego and Ariane Dewey.

Like Me and You: Words and music by Raffi and Debi Pike. Text copyright © 1985 by Homeland Publishing, a division of Troubadour Records Ltd. Illustrations copyright © 1994 by Lillian Hoban.

One Light, One Sun: Words and music by Raffi. Text copyright © 1988 by Troubadour Learning, a division of Troubadour Records Ltd. Illustrations copyright © 1988 by Eugenie Fernandes.

Shake My Sillies Out: Music by Raffi. Words by Bert and Bonnie Simpson. Text copyright © 1987 by Troubadour Learning, a division of Troubadour Records Ltd. Illustrations copyright © 1987 by David Allender.

Spider on the Floor: Words and music by Bill Russell. Text copyright © 1976 by Egos Anonymous (PRO). Illustrations copyright © 1993 by True Kelley.

Tingalayo: Text copyright © 1989 by Troubadour Learning, a division of Troubadour Records Ltd. Illustrations copyright © 1989 by Kate Duke.

Wheels on the Bus: Text copyright © 1988 by Troubadour Learning, a division of Troubadour Records Ltd. Illustrations copyright © 1988 by Sylvie Wickstrom.

Published by Crown Publishers, Inc., a Random House company,
201 East 50th Street, New York, New York 10022
CROWN is a trademark of Crown Publishers, Inc.
RAFFI SONGS TO READ and **SONGS TO READ** are registered trademarks of
Troubadour Learning, a division of Troubadour Records Ltd.

Library of Congress Cataloging-in-Publication Data
Raffi.
Raffi's top 10 songs to read
p. cm.
Contents: Baby Beluga—Down by the bay—Everything grows—Five little ducks—Like me and you—One light, one sun—Shake my sillies out—Spider on the floor—Tingalayo—Wheels on the bus.
Summary: Includes lyrics, music, illustrations, and a suggested activity for each of ten children's songs.
1. Children's songs—Texts. [1. Songs.] I. Title. II. Title: Top 10 songs to read. III. Title: Top ten songs to read.
PZ8.3.R124Rag 1995 95-196 782.42164 0268–dc20

ISBN: 0-517-70907-4

Manufactured in the United States of America

10 9 8 7 6 5 4 3 2 1

Raffi's Top 10 Songs to Read®

Pictures by
David Allender, Jose Aruego & Ariane Dewey,
Kate Duke, Eugenie Fernandes, Lillian Hoban,
True Kelley, Bruce McMillan, Nadine Bernard Westcott,
Sylvie Kantorovitz Wickstrom, and Ashley Wolff

Crown Publishers, Inc., New York

One of my greatest rewards as a children's entertainer has been discovering how naturally and easily young children respond to music. They love to hear their favorite songs over and over and they quickly become familiar with the words. As children listen and sing, they are learning the concepts that underlie beginning reading: story, sequence of events, rhyme, and rhythm.

The repetition and predictable pattern of my songs make them "singable" and easy for children to remember. The same qualities make them readable, too.

This collection of **Songs to Read**® is a natural bridge between singing and reading. Once children know a song, they find it's fun and easy to follow it in pictures and in words.

Whether you read along or sing along, my **Songs to Read**® will provide both pleasure and real learning. Enjoy sharing it with your children!

Raffi

contents

Baby Beluga 8

Down by the Bay 12

Everything Grows 16

Five Little Ducks 19

Like Me and You 22

One Light, One Sun 26

Shake My Sillies Out 29

Spider on the Floor 32

Tingalayo 36

Wheels on the Bus 40

Activities 44

Baby Beluga

Pictures by Ashley Wolff

Baby beluga in the deep blue sea,
Swim so wild and you swim so free.
Heaven above and the sea below,
And a little white whale on the go.

Baby beluga, baby beluga,
Is the water warm? Is your mama home,
With you so happy?

Way down yonder where the dolphins play,
Where you dive and splash all day,
Waves roll in and the waves roll out.
See the water squirtin' out of your spout.

Baby beluga, oh, baby beluga,
Sing your little song, sing for all your friends.
We like to hear you.

When it's dark, you're home and fed.
Curl up snug in your water bed.
Moon is shining and the stars are out.
Good night, little whale, good night.

Baby beluga, oh, baby beluga,
With tomorrow's sun, another day's begun.
You'll soon be waking.

Baby beluga in the deep blue sea,
Swim so wild and you swim so free.
Heaven above and the sea below,
And a little white whale on the go.
You're just a little white whale on the go.

Baby Beluga

Ba - by be - lu - ga in the deep blue sea, Swim so wild and you swim so free.

Heav - en a - bove and the sea be - low, And a little white whale on the go.

Ba - by be - lu - ga, ba - by be - lu - ga,

Is the wa - ter warm? Is your ma - ma home, With you so hap - py?

2. Way down yonder where the dolphins play,
Where you dive and splash all day,
Waves roll in and the waves roll out.
See the water squirtin' out of your spout.

Baby beluga, oh, baby beluga,
Sing your little song, sing for all your friends.
We like to hear you.

3. When it's dark, you're home and fed.
Curl up snug in your water bed.
Moon is shining and the stars are out.
Good night, little whale, good night.

Baby beluga, oh, baby beluga,
With tomorrow's sun, another day's begun.
You'll soon be waking.

4. Baby beluga in the deep blue sea,
Swim so wild and you swim so free.
Heaven above and the sea below,
And a little white whale on the go.
You're just a little white whale on the go.

Down by the Bay

Pictures by Nadine Bernard Westcott

Down by the bay, where the watermelons grow,
Back to my home I dare not go.
For if I do my mother will say,
"Did you ever see a goose kissing a moose,
Down by the bay?"

Down by the bay, where the watermelons grow,
Back to my home I dare not go.
For if I do my mother will say,
"Did you ever see a whale with a polka-dot tail,
Down by the bay?"

Down by the bay, where the watermelons grow,
Back to my home I dare not go.
For if I do my mother will say,
"Did you ever see a fly wearing a tie,
Down by the bay?"

Down by the bay, where the watermelons grow,
Back to my home I dare not go.
For if I do my mother will say,
"Did you ever see a bear combing his hair,
Down by the bay?"

Down by the bay, where the watermelons grow,
Back to my home I dare not go.
For if I do my mother will say,
"Did you ever see llamas eating their pajamas,
Down by the bay?"

Down by the bay, where the
    watermelons grow,
Back to my home I dare not go.
For if I do my mother will say,
"Did you ever have a time when
    you couldn't make a rhyme,
Down by the bay?"

Down by the Bay

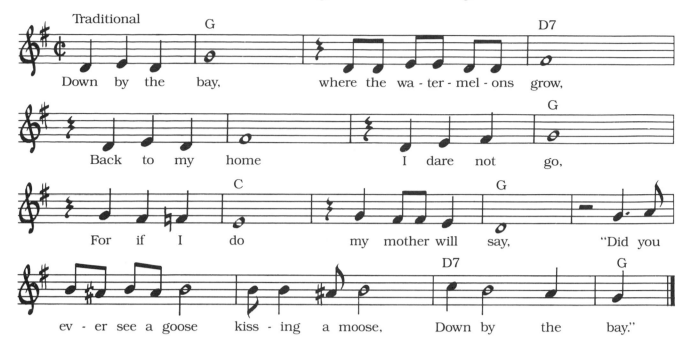

Traditional

Down by the bay, where the wa-ter-mel-ons grow,

Back to my home I dare not go,

For if I do my mother will say, "Did you

ev-er see a goose kiss-ing a moose, Down by the bay."

2. "Did you ever see a whale with a polka-dot tail…"
3. "Did you ever see a fly wearing a tie…"
4. "Did you ever see a bear combing his hair…"
5. "Did you ever see llamas eating their pajamas…"
6. "Did you ever have a time when you couldn't make a rhyme…Down by the bay."

Everything Grows

Pictures by Bruce McMillan

Everything grows and grows.
Babies do, animals too.
Everything grows.
Everything grows and grows.
Sisters do, brothers too.
Everything grows.

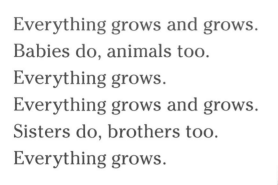

A blade of grass, fingers and toes,
Hair on my head, a red, red rose.
Everything grows, anyone knows,
That's how it goes.

Everything grows and grows.
Babies do, animals too.
Everything grows.

16

Everything grows and grows.
Sisters do, brothers too.
Everything grows.

Food on the farm, fish in the sea,
Birds in the air, leaves on the tree.
Everything grows, anyone knows,
That's how it goes.

That's how it goes, under the sun.
That's how it goes, under the rain.
Everything grows, anyone knows,
That's how it goes.

Yes, everything grows and grows.
Babies do, animals too.
Everything grows.
Everything grows and grows.
Sisters do, brothers too.
Everything grows.
Mamas do, papas too.
Everything grows.

17

Everything Grows

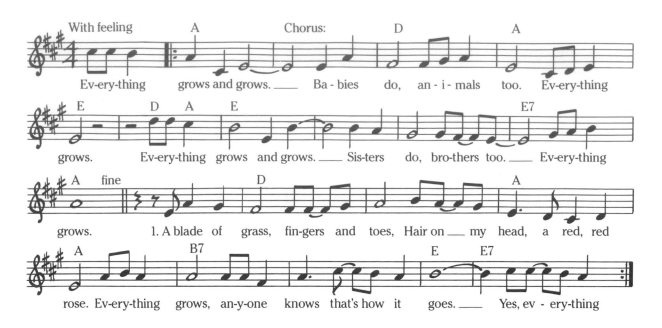

With feeling

Ev-ery-thing grows and grows.___ Ba-bies do, an-i-mals too. Ev-ery-thing grows.

Ev-ery-thing grows and grows.___ Sis-ters do, bro-thers too.___ Ev-ery-thing grows.

1. A blade of grass, fin-gers and toes, Hair on___ my head, a red, red rose. Ev-ery-thing grows, an-y-one knows that's how it goes.___ Yes, ev-ery-thing

2. Food on the farm, fish in the sea,
Birds in the air, leaves on the tree.
Everything grows, anyone knows,
That's how it goes.

3. That's how it goes, under the sun.
That's how it goes, under the rain.
Everything grows, anyone knows.
That's how it goes.

Five Little Ducks

Pictures by Jose Aruego and Ariane Dewey

Five little ducks went out one day,
Over the hills and far away.
Mother Duck said,
"Quack, quack, quack, quack."
But only four little ducks came back.

Four little ducks went out one day,
Over the hills and far away.
Mother Duck said,
"Quack, quack, quack, quack."
But only three little ducks came back.

Three little ducks went out one day,
Over the hills and far away.
Mother Duck said,
"Quack, quack, quack, quack."
But only two little ducks came back.

Two little ducks went out one day,
Over the hills and far away.
Mother Duck said,
"Quack, quack, quack, quack."
But only one little duck came back.

One little duck went out one day,
Over the hills and far away.
Mother Duck said,
"Quack, quack, quack, quack."
But none of the five little ducks came back.

Sad Mother Duck went out one day,
Over the hills and far away.
Mother Duck said,
"Quack, quack, quack, quack!"
And all of the five little ducks came back.

Five Little Ducks

Brightly

Five lit- tle ducks went out one day, O- ver the hills and far a- way. Mo- ther duck said, "Quack, quack, quack, quack!" But on- ly four lit- tle ducks came back.

2. Four little ducks went out one day...
   But only three little ducks came back.

3. Three little ducks went out one day...
   But only two little ducks came back.

4. Two little ducks went out one day...
   But only one little duck came back.

5. One little duck went out one day...
   But none of the five little ducks came back.

6. Sad Mother Duck went out one day...
   And all of the five little ducks came back.

Like Me and You

Pictures by Lillian Hoban

Janet lives in England, Pierre lives in France,
Bonnie lives in Canada.
Ahmed lives in Egypt, Moshe lives in Israel,
Bruce lives in Australia.

Ching lives in China, Olga lives in Russia,
Ingrid lives in Germany.
Gita lives in India, Pablo lives in Spain,
José lives in Colombia.

And each one is much like another.
A child of a mother and a father.
A very special son or daughter.
A lot like me and you.

Koji lives in Japan,
Nina lives in Chile,
Farida lives in Pakistan.
Zosia lives in Poland,
Manual lives in Brazil,
Maria lives in Italy.

Kofi lives in Ghana, Rahim lives in Iran,
Rosa lives in Paraguay.
Meja lives in Kenya, Demetri lives in Greece,
Sue lives in America.

And each one is much like another.
A child of a mother and a father.
A very special son or daughter.
A lot like me and you.

Like Me and You

1. Jan-et lives in Eng-land, Pierre lives in France, Bonnie lives in Can-a-da._

Ah-med lives in E-gypt, Mo-she lives in Is-ra-el, Bruce lives in Aus-tra-li-a._

Ching lives in Chi-na, Ol-ga lives in Rus-sia,_

In-grid lives in Ger-man-y._ Gi-ta lives in In-di-a, Pab-lo lives in Spain, Jo-

sé lives in Co-lom-bi-a._ And each one is much like an-

oth-er._ A child of a moth-er and a fa-ther._ A ver-y spe-cial son or

daugh-ter._ A lot like me and you._

CODA

(Hum)

2. Koji lives in Japan, Nina lives in Chile,
   Farida lives in Pakistan.
   Zosia lives in Poland, Manual lives in Brazil,
   Maria lives in Italy.
   Kofi lives in Ghana, Rahim lives in Iran,
   Rosa lives in Paraguay.
   Meja lives in Kenya, Demetri lives in Greece,
   Sue lives in America.

Repeat chorus

25

One Light, One Sun

Pictures by Eugenie Fernandes

One light, one sun,
One sun lighting everyone.
One world turning,
One world turning everyone.

One world, one home,
One world home for everyone.
One dream, one song,
One song heard by everyone.

One love, one heart,
One heart warming everyone.
One hope, one joy,
One love filling everyone.

One light, one sun,
One sun lighting everyone.

One light warming everyone.

One Light, One Sun

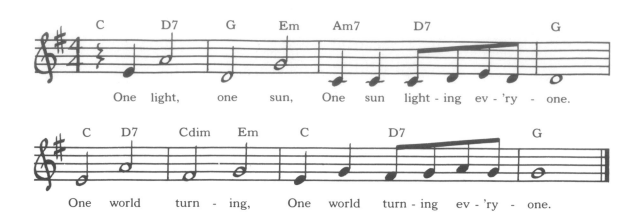

One light, one sun, One sun light-ing ev-'ry-one.

One world turn-ing, One world turn-ing ev-'ry-one.

2. One world, one home,
   One world home for everyone.
   One dream, one song,
   One song heard by everyone.

3. One love, one heart,
   One heart warming everyone.
   One hope, one joy,
   One love filling everyone.

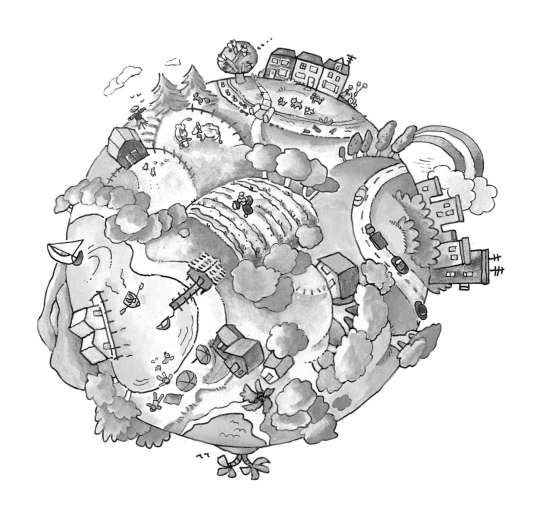

Shake My Sillies Out

Pictures by David Allender

Gotta shake, shake, shake my sillies out,
Shake, shake, shake my sillies out,
Shake, shake, shake my sillies out,
And wiggle my waggles away.

Gotta clap, clap, clap my crazies out,
Clap, clap, clap my crazies out,
Clap, clap, clap my crazies out,
And wiggle my waggles away.

Gotta jump, jump, jump my jiggles out,
Jump, jump, jump my jiggles out,
Jump, jump, jump my jiggles out,
And wiggle my waggles away.

Gotta yawn, yawn, yawn my sleepies out,
Yawn, yawn, yawn my sleepies out,
Yawn, yawn, yawn my sleepies out,
And wiggle my waggles away.

Gotta shake, shake, shake my sillies out,
Shake, shake, shake my sillies out,
Shake, shake, shake my sillies out,
And wiggle my waggles away.

Shake My Sillies Out

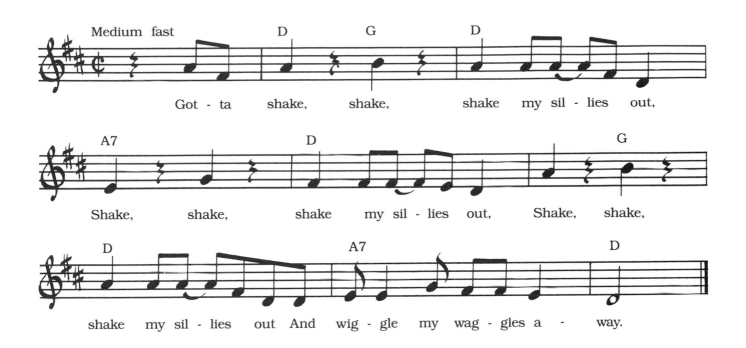

Medium fast

Got - ta shake, shake, shake my sil - lies out,
Shake, shake, shake my sil - lies out, Shake, shake,
shake my sil - lies out And wig - gle my wag - gles a - way.

2. Gotta clap, clap, clap my crazies out,
Clap, clap, clap my crazies out,
Clap, clap, clap my crazies out,
And wiggle my waggles away.

3. Gotta jump, jump, jump my jiggles out...

4. (Slower) Gotta yawn, yawn, yawn my sleepies out...

5. Gotta shake, shake, shake my sillies out...

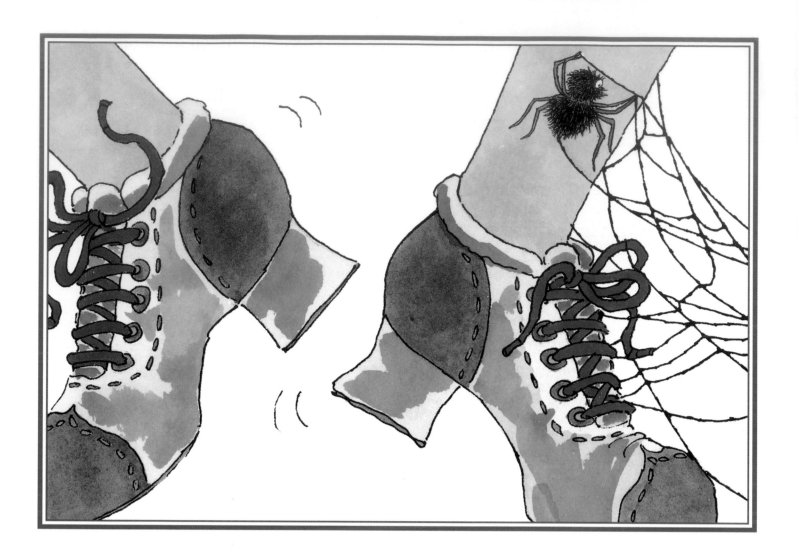

Spider on the Floor

Pictures by True Kelley

There's a spider on the floor, on the floor.
There's a spider on the floor, on the floor.
Who could ask for any more than a spider on the floor?
There's a spider on the floor, on the floor.

Now the spider's on my leg, on my leg.
Oh, the spider's on my leg, on my leg.
Oh, he's really big! This old spider on my leg.
There's a spider on my leg, on my leg.

Now the spider's on my stomach, on my stomach.
Oh, the spider's on my stomach, on my stomach.
Oh, he's just a dumb old lummock,
   this old spider on my stomach.
There's a spider on my stomach, on my stomach.

Now the spider's on my neck, on my neck.
Oh, the spider's on my neck, on my neck.
Oh, I'm gonna be a wreck, I've got a spider on my neck.
There's a spider on my neck, on my neck.

Now the spider's on my face, on my face.
Oh, the spider's on my face, on my face.
Oh, what a big disgrace, I've got a spider on my face.
There's a spider on my face, on my face.

Now the spider's on my head, on my head.
Oh, the spider's on my head, on my head.
Oh, I wish that I were dead, I've got a spider on my head,
There's a spider on my head, on my head.

But he jumps off...

There's a spider on the floor, on the floor.
There's a spider on the floor, on the floor.
Who could ask for any more than a spider on the floor?
There's a spider on the floor, on the floor...

Spider on the Floor

1. There's a spi-der on the floor, on the floor. There's a spi-der on the floor, on the floor. Who could ask for an-y more than a spi-der on the floor? There's a

1.-6. spi — der on the floor, on the floor. *2.* Now the floor.

2. Now the spider's on my leg, on my leg.
Oh, the spider's on my leg, on my leg.
Oh, he's really big! This old spider on my leg.
There's a spider on my leg, on my leg.

3. Now the spider's on my stomach, on my stomach.
Oh, the spider's on my stomach, on my stomach.
Oh, he's just a dumb old lummock, this old spider on my stomach.
There's a spider on my stomach, on my stomach.

4. Now the spider's on my neck, on my neck.
Oh, the spider's on my neck, on my neck.
Oh, I'm gonna be a wreck, I've got a spider on my neck.
There's a spider on my neck, on my neck.

5. Now the spider's on my face, on my face.
Oh, the spider's on my face, on my face.
Oh, what a big disgrace, I've got a spider on my face.
There's a spider on my face, on my face.

6. Now the spider's on my head, on my head.
Oh, the spider's on my head, on my head.
Oh, I wish that I were dead, I've got a spider on my head.
There's a spider on my head, on my head.

Spoken: But he jumps off...

7. *Repeat 1st Verse*

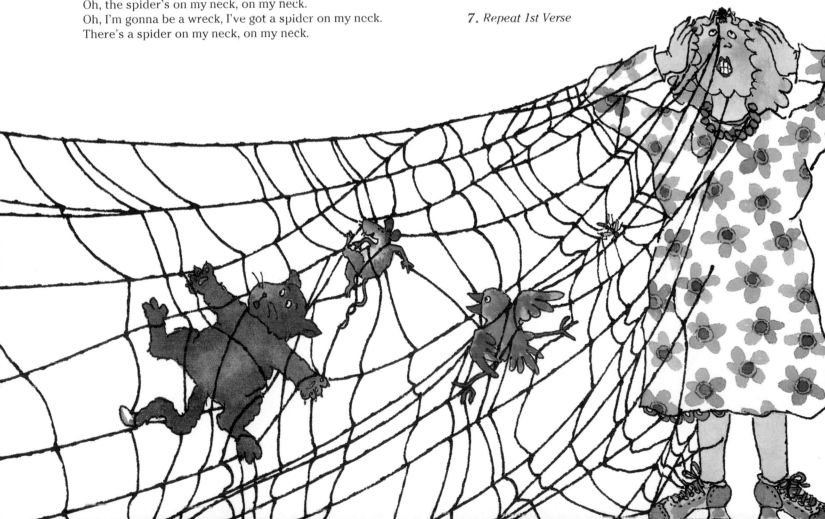

Tingalayo

Pictures by Kate Duke

Tingalayo, come, little donkey, come.
Tingalayo, come, little donkey, come.

Me donkey fast, me donkey slow,
Me donkey come and me donkey go.
Me donkey fast, me donkey slow,
Me donkey come and me donkey go.

Tingalayo, come, little donkey, come.
Tingalayo, come, little donkey, come.

Me donkey hee, me donkey haw,
Me donkey sleep in a bed of straw.
Me donkey hee, me donkey haw,
Me donkey sleep in a bed of straw.

Tingalayo, come, little donkey, come.
Tingalayo, come, little donkey, come.

Me donkey dance, me donkey sing,
Me donkey wearin' a diamond ring.
Me donkey dance, me donkey sing,
Me donkey wearin' a diamond ring.

Tingalayo, come, little donkey, come.
Tingalayo, come, little donkey, come.

Me donkey swim, me donkey ski,
Me donkey dress elegantly.
Me donkey swim, me donkey ski,
Me donkey dress elegantly.

Tingalayo, come, little donkey, come.
Tingalayo, come, little donkey, come.

Tingalayo

Chorus

Tin- ga- lay- o, come, lit- tle don- key, come. Tin- ga-

Verse

lay- o, come, lit- tle don- key, come. Me don- key

fast, me don-key slow, Me don-key come and me don-key go. Me don-key

fast, me don-key slow, Me don-key come and me don-key go.

2. Me donkey hee, me donkey haw,
   Me donkey sleep in a bed of straw.

3. Me donkey dance, me donkey sing,
   Me donkey wearin' a diamond ring.

4. Me donkey swim, me donkey ski,
   Me donkey dress elegantly.

Wheels on the Bus

Pictures by Sylvie Kantorovitz Wickstrom

The wheels on the bus
go round and round,
round and round,
round and round.
The wheels on the bus
go round and round,
all around the town.

The wipers on the bus
go *swish swish swish,*
swish swish swish,
swish swish swish.
The wipers on the bus
go *swish swish swish,*
all around the town.

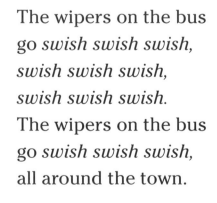

The driver on the bus
goes "Move on back!
Move on back,
move on back!"
The driver on the bus
goes "Move on back!"
all around the town.

The people on the bus
go up and down,
up and down,
up and down.
The people on the bus
go up and down,
all around the town.

The horn on the bus
goes *beep beep beep,*
beep beep beep,
beep beep beep.
The horn on the bus
goes *beep beep beep,*
all around the town.

The baby on the bus
goes "Wah wah wah,
wah wah wah,
wah wah wah."
The baby on the bus
goes "Wah wah wah,"
all around the town.

The parents on the bus
go "Shh shh shh,
shh shh shh,
shh shh shh."
The parents on the bus
go "Shh shh shh,"
all around the town.

The wheels on the bus
go round and round,
round and round,
round and round.
The wheels on the bus
go round and round,
all around the town.

Wheels on the Bus

1. The wheels on the bus go round and round, round and round, round and round, The wheels on the bus go round and round, all a - round the town.

2. The wipers on the bus
   go *swish swish swish*...

3. The driver on the bus
   goes "Move on back!"...

4. The people on the bus
   go up and down...

5. The horn on the bus
   goes *beep, beep, beep*...

6. The baby on the bus
   goes "Wah, wah, wah"...

7. The parents on the bus
   go "Shh, shh, shh"...

Activities

Baby Beluga

This is a "bright and tuneful love song for a baby whale," says Raffi.

• Look in your local library for recordings of whale songs. Try to imitate some of the sounds that whales make when they communicate. Make up a song of your own.

Down by the Bay

The tales in this song get wilder and wilder as each child tries to outdo the other in rhyme and imagination.

• Make up verses of your own using names of animals and familiar objects. Take turns completing the lines with your friends—and be as imaginative as you can!

Everything Grows

This song celebrates the natural growth and change that happen in the world.

• Try planting some beans or other fast-growing seeds and keep a photo journal of their progress.

• Look around you and make a list of all the things you see that are living. Then make a list of objects around you that are made of things that were once living (hint: paper, a wooden table or chair, leather shoes).

Five Little Ducks

This song offers a good excuse to quack. But Raffi warns that sometimes it's hard to stop quacking once you start! Get quacking!

• As you sing and quack along, make up simple hand actions to accompany the song:

Five little ducks went out one day.
Hold up five fingers.

Over the hills and far away.
Make a wavy motion with your hand.

Mother Duck said, "Quack, quack, quack, quack."
Put your hands together to make a beak.

But only four little ducks came back.
Hold up four fingers, then make a running motion with them.

Like Me and You

"When we understand all that we have in common with others," says Raffi, "our differences become things to celebrate."

• A pen pal is a great way to realize how much we have in common with others. Try getting involved in a pen pal program at school, or ask your teacher to help arrange a small one with another class.

• Make up new verses to the song using names of your friends. Sing about the country where each friend's family comes from or the name of the street they live on (e.g., "Paula lives on Maple Avenue").

One Light, One Sun

This song teaches us that, no matter how different, we are all related in that we share the same sun, the same earth, the same bounties of nature.

• How many people are in your family? Draw a picture of each one. Make a list of the activities that each family member does in the morning, in the afternoon, and at night. Are there special activities that they do each week? Each year? Put the list next to the person's picture in a scrapbook and share it with your family.

Shake My Sillies Out

Shake your sillies out with some musical accompaniment of your own!

• Put beans, rice, buttons, or other small objects into unbreakable containers with lids (margarine tubs, yogurt cups, or plastic bottles). Shake the objects to the beat and see what different sounds you can make.

• Cut out magazine pictures of things that shake or jump. Make a book out of what you've collected.

Spider on the Floor

Singing this song is a fun way to learn the parts of the body.

• As you sing this song, touch the part of your body that you are singing about. Touch your leg, stomach, neck, face, and head.

• Or make up new verses to the song and name even more body parts as you go along.

Tingalayo

When you sing this song, you'll want to clap along with the catchy melody and rhythm!

• Sing the words below. Clap when you see the symbol *.

(Sing words in italics. Clap for *)

Me donkey hee,
*Me donkey **
Me donkey haw,
*Me donkey **
Me donkey sleep in a bed of straw.
*Me donkey * * * * * * **
or
Me donkey hee,
** * * hee,*
Me donkey haw,
** * * haw,*
Me donkey sleep in a bed of straw.
** * * sleep in a bed of straw.*

Wheels on the Bus

This song is so much fun you'll want to teach it to a friend!

• Add new lyrics to the song: e.g., "The lights on the bus go blink, blink, blink."

• Create a new song: e.g., "The cows on the farm go moo, moo, moo." For a Halloween version, try "The ghosts in the house go boo, boo, boo."

45